For Pandora
J.N.

For Sam's Mum
P. H.

First published in Great Britain in 1999.
This edition first published in 2001
by Egmont Children's Books Limited,
a division of Egmont Holding Limited,
239 Kensington High Street, London W8 6SA.

Text copyright © Jenny Nimmo 1999
Illustrations copyright © Paul Howard 1999
The author and illustrator have asserted their moral rights

ISBN 0 7497 4711 0

A CIP catalogue record for this title is available from the British Library

Printed in UAE

1 3 5 7 9 10 8 6 4 2

The
Strongest Girl
In the World

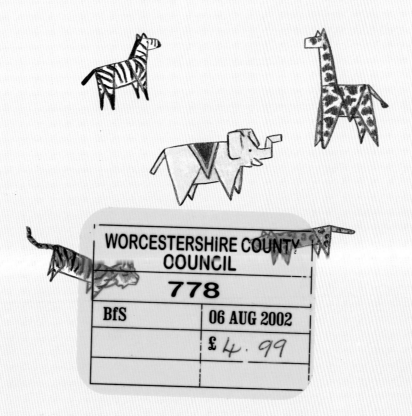

Jenny Nimmo
Illustrated by
Paul Howard

EGMONT CHILDREN'S BOOKS

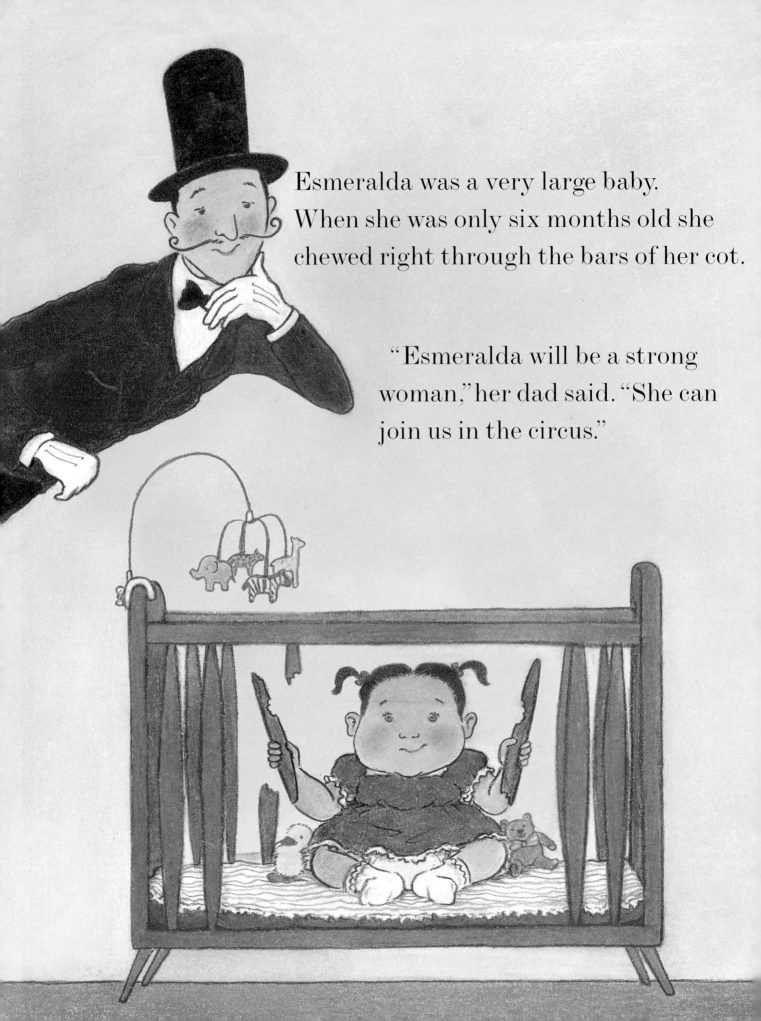

Esmeralda was a very large baby. When she was only six months old she chewed right through the bars of her cot.

"Esmeralda will be a strong woman," her dad said. "She can join us in the circus."

When Esmeralda was four years old she could lift an armchair.

Her mum made her a leopard-skin top and a frilly skirt.

But the children-next-door wouldn't play with Esmeralda.

"You're a giant," they said. "You would hurt us."

And they wouldn't let Esmeralda hold their toys.
"You're too clumsy," they said. "You would break them."

When Esmeralda was six she could carry
her mum and dad on her shoulders.

The children-next-door wouldn't even let
Esmeralda go near their cat.

"You're too strong," they said. "You would crush her."

When Esmeralda was seven her mum and dad said,
"Esmeralda, soon you can join our circus act.
You are a strong-woman now."

They thought this would make their daughter happy.
But Esmeralda didn't want to be a strong-woman.
She wanted to be an acrobat or a tightrope walker.
She didn't like eating meat every day, or wearing animal
skins or lifting weights.

"Strong-women eat meat to make them grow," her dad said. "They lift weights to keep them strong and they wear animal skins to show they are as tough as lions."

So Esmeralda ate her meat and lifted weights and wore a leopard-skin, but she was very unhappy. She grew so big the children-next-door ran away from her.

Alone in her room Esmeralda made beautiful paper
animals and sang to them.
They were her only friends.

But the children-next-door called out, "Esmeralda
sings like a frog!" never guessing that she had gentle,
clever fingers and a heart of gold.

In the summer Esmeralda and
her family went on tour.
They performed in cities
all round the world.

Esmeralda carried her
parents on her shoulders.

She threw them in the
air and caught them.

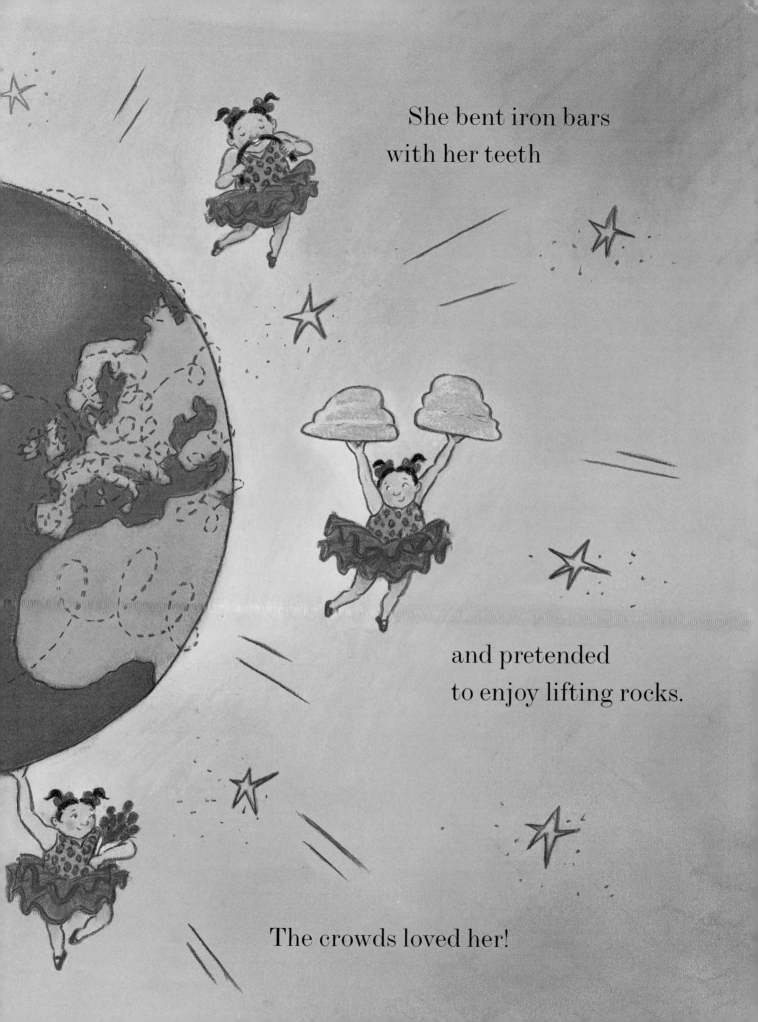

She bent iron bars
with her teeth

and pretended
to enjoy lifting rocks.

The crowds loved her!

But at night when Mum and Dad were sleeping in their brightly-painted caravan, Esmeralda would gaze at the moon and think about the children-next-door.

When autumn came the tour ended and the family returned home.

Mum and Dad cooked a special supper to celebrate their first night home, but Esmeralda didn't enjoy it. When she went to bed, she didn't sing to her paper animals. She was too sad.

In the morning Esmeralda ran to peep in the garden next door.

The children had a new baby sister. Esmeralda longed to hold her, but the children shouted, "Go away, Esmeralda. You'll frighten the baby."

The next day a wind swept into the village.
Esmeralda ran outside and watched the clouds tearing
through the sky. The wind was as fierce and strong
as she was.

"Come and play with me," she cried. "No one else will."

But the wind rushed past Esmeralda and into the
branches of the tree next door. The tree shuddered
and a great branch cracked.

The baby-next-door was fast asleep in her pram under the tree. The children-next-door looked out of the window and saw the branch was going to crush their baby. They all rushed out of the house, but they were too scared to go near the tree.

Esmeralda leapt over the wall and caught the branch as it fell. She pushed the branch away from the baby and it crashed to the ground beside the pram. Esmeralda felt her great strength leaving her.

The children-next-door tiptoed over to the girl lying in the grass.

"She doesn't look frightening any more," they said. Esmeralda's dad ran out to see what had happened.

"She saved our baby," called the children-next-door. "How can we thank her?"

Esmeralda's mum put her in bed and waited for her to get better.

The doctor came and shook his head. "It seems Esmeralda doesn't want to get strong again," he said.

Esmeralda lay in bed all winter.
She never saw the children-next-door skating,
tobogganing and snowballing.

Sometimes they looked up
at Esmeralda's window. They
wondered where she was.
They missed her.

When the trees began to blossom, Mum said, "We can't go on tour without Esmeralda. What shall we do?"

"Perhaps it's time we asked the children-next-door," suggested Dad.

The children-next-door were sorry to hear Esmeralda was still ill and went to visit her.

They saw all the paper animals so neatly and cleverly made.

"How beautiful," they whispered. "We wish we could make paper animals."

The children crept close to Esmeralda. They put their toys, their cat and their baby on her bed.

"Please get strong, Esmeralda," they said. "We want you to come and play with us."

Esmeralda gave a tiny smile. Only the baby saw it.

The next day, Esmeralda sat up in bed.

"What a lovely day, "she said. "What's for breakfast?"

Then Esmeralda gathered up her paper animals, opened the window and threw them into the air.

"For you!" she cried to the children-next-door.

"Hurrah!" they shouted as they ran to catch the floating creatures. "Esmeralda is well again."

Esmeralda is still with the circus but she's not the strong woman any more.

Every summer she goes round the world with her mum and dad.

She swings high on the trapeze and walks the tightrope.

The crowds stare in amazement and gasp at her bravery.

Esmeralda loves it.

But in the autumn she comes home to play with the children-next-door.

They say she's the best friend they've ever had.

Koala and the Flower by Mary Murphy
0 7497 4407 3

I Don't Want to Sleep Alone
by Alison Ritchie and Cathy Gale
0 7497 4661 0

A Story for Hippo
by Simon Puttock and Alison Bartlett
0 7497 4022 1

Mr Wolf's Pancakes by Jan Fearnley
0 7497 3559 7

Cat's Colours by Jane Cabrera
0 7497 3120 6

Dog's Day by Jane Cabrera
0 7497 4392 1

I wish I were a dog by Lydia Monks
0 7497 3803 0

The Three Little Wolves and the Big Bad Pig
by Eugene Trivizas and Helen Oxenbury
0 7497 2505 2

And they're all only £4.99